Eradication of Caste

FanatiXx Publication
ISO 9001:2015 Certified

FanatiXx Publication
AM/56, Basanti Colony, Rourkela 769012, Odisha
ISO 9001:2015 CERTIFIED
Website: *www.fanatixx.in*

"Eradication of Caste"

By: Shruti Tayal

ISBN: 978-93-89106-45-9

Anthology of Articles 1st Edition

Book Formatting: Saizal Gupta

Cover Design: Sagar Samal

Spread
Smile

Disclaimer

The anthology is a work of non-fiction. We have tried our best to check plagiarism in the write-ups of all the authors contributing to this book. However, if something has escaped and plagiarism is detected at a later date, we shall not be held liable for the same. We have guided our authors to contribute original and unplagiarized pieces.

Acknowledgement

The completion of this anthology would not have been possible without the incredible rate of work and help of our co-authors. Every co-author has put his/her utmost efforts for the completion of this project. Immense thanks to all the co-authors who gave their precious time for this book.

The anthology is flawlessly compiled and edited by Shruti Tayal.
Bunch of thanks to our publishers FanatiXx Publications, for helping me in every step. Without you, this would not have been possible.

Big Thanks to my teachers and friends for their blessings and love.
Above all, Thanks to My parents and Inspiration who are always there for me.

5

SHRUTI TAYAL

Compiler & Editor

Daughter of Mr. Brijmohan Tayal and Mrs. Babita Tayal was brought up in Palwal, Haryana. She is 18 years old. Currently, she is pursuing her graduation in physics. She started writing almost two years ago to follow her instincts, and now she traps her readers with her words. The purpose of her life is to make people realize their worth.

She is a true example of determinant and hard working. She has worked in many anthologies as a co-author, promoter, and manager. Her debut compilation **'Petals of Life'** has also been published in which she has worked with 60 writers.
Alongside, she is also the founder of **"Spread Smile"**, a platform where she gives a nudge to all budding writers and helps them get published.
Also, she works at FanatiXx as a video designer.

Besides writing, she loves cooking, reading and reviewing novels, etc.
She wishes to be a novelist someday.

You may contact her via---
Email: shrutitayal268@gmail.com
Instagram: @spread_smile_shruti_skye | @shruti_khushbu
Twitter: @shrutiskye
Facebook:
https://www.facebook.com/shruti.tayal.1004

Compiler's Note

"There is always a step small enough from where we are to get us to where we want to be. If we take that small step, there's always another we can take, and eventually, a goal thought to be too far to reach becomes achievable."

— Ellen Langer

All readers are warmly welcomed. **Spread Smile** presents ***"Eradication of Caste in Modern world"*** to every citizen of this nation. The main objective of bringing 40 authors together is just not writing and releasing a book, but it's to bring a change in our society. This book of 40 articles is a small step against casteism and discrimination. One and all wordsmith has designated/prescribed their little by little for the completion of this ***"Step"***.

I know, many of you will claim that at this time, casteism doesn't exist. My dear readers, explore this world, explore the things you're lagging behind, visit tribal areas and villages; you'll come to know that casteism still exists. Our parents, grandparents have accepted social media instead of a pigeon to convey their messages, but they aren't accepting that we are all the same, we are all humans.

Apart from this, you'd have seen people fighting over a system called *" **Reservation system"**. This system is always a part of our conversation when we talk about casteism. Unreserved people demand it to be removed, and reserved ones use it for their benefits. Not only reserved, but even unreserved ones also create the fake profiles that they belong to reserved.

• *Have you ever thought of which the reservation is the result?*

• *Have you ever wondered how we can change things?*

• *Ever thought what's the role of religion in casteism?*

• *Is casteism the only reason for which we discriminate?*

• *How can we change the mentality of our parents, grandparents, and society?*

• *How have our surnames and castes become our identity?*

• *Does untouchability still exist?*

• *Why don't we allow some people to be the priest of a temple?*

• *How does casteism affect us politically?*

• *When do we start treating everyone equally?*

• *Why do we discriminate when we know that we all are humans?*

Many questions, many problems but the solution is one, i.e., **Eradication of Caste**. Accept everyone as a human, not with a badge of Caste, Color, Sex, etc.

Read this book out full of 40 articles written by wonderful authors! You'll get to know your answers.

"Humans are being harassed on the name of Caste,

Let us come together to eradicate the Caste."

#HappyReading

Thanks & Regards

Shruti Tayal (Skye)

Note: *Criticizers and Appreciators can mail us on shrutitayal268@gmail.com or spreadsmile28@gmail.com*

Supporters can join us and post a tweet against casteism using hashtags #EradicationOfCaste #CasteFreeIndia

Co-Author's

Vrushali
Shaikh Sohel
Anjali Jha
Akul Agarwal

Akankshya Mishra
Aakash Karanjavkar
Ch. Mahesh Babu
Shrangarika Sharma

Sourav Rathour
Naina Mishra
Satbir Singh Patel
Sulagna Chakraborty

Sweta Kumari
Hafizur Rahman
Harsh Bhadoriya
Apurv Bhardwaj

Udisha Singh
Anisha Garg
Ritika Dasgupta
Madan English Lecturer

Harshita Sevaldasani
Soumick Mukherjee
Kaushik Singh maravi
Suchismita Ghoshal

Tejaswi Vajinepalli
Mandeep Singh Chawla
Bala Sundaram . P
Shivani Khemani

Mohan Sharma
Deeksha R. Adiga
Rubal Choudhary
Sanchari Das

Siddharth Sharma

Ankur payar

Amrita singh

Siddhesh Shimpukade

Vishal Bhatiya
Tarun Vij भारतीय
Risha Jagga
Vaishno Singh

Eradication of Caste

The Wounded Society

"Cried to take the first breath
A baby was born in a hut
unaware of the discriminations
puking on earth
She was forced to gamble for her life
from now to forever!"

These lines fairly describe how life for few people can be miserable here in India where caste is deeply rooted in the veins of society. Casteism is like a leach thriving on inferiority and unfair treatments. From the moment we have born to the last breath we take, everything exists in the bubble we call as caste and very few were brave enough to voice their opinion against it. Their pledge was heard and was also applied, but was all the measures still necessary in this 21st century? Let's find out about it elaborately.

History says that earlier there was no caste but just occupations. People were given different jobs to perform. Some of them were good and some were brutally disgusting. But these jobs they just didn't survive to just for a man, but it was passed on generation to generation and remained in the family. Later, the group of such specified workers was carved into castes. At present, Caste is included in the birth certificate and also in the death certificate. This is laughable. From the admissions to the kindergarten to jobs, Caste is mentioned and asked everywhere. Looking to the scenarios now, I wonder why that field is still dangling in the forms? Don't these educational institutes should set an example of equality? Shouldn't the workplaces hire talents and not reserved seats? Shouldn't the politics be composed of leaders and not the forced people on whom the other powerful person can thrive. Shouldn't the opportunities be given to desirables rather than reservations?

Many questions but I bet nobody can stand to answer them. Everyone knows that caste, which was earlier considered to be bad treatments, has now taken a toll around and is creating hindrances in the living of this generation. If we want to change this, then we must change the ways of the admissions and selection processes. The admission must be purely merit-based and selection must be purely justified. Elections must be on capabilities and assignments must be on deserving. And all these can be achieved when we erase one factor from all the forms: Religion/Caste/Creed/Sub-caste and god knows what else they call to it. This will facilitate the credible to appear and desirables to get benefited. When a person is hired fully just on his achievements and credibility, this will also benefit the organization. The educational seats will be given on merit, and people will restore their belief in government again!

"When she was just a person
Not recognized by her caste,
but by her achievements
She was truly risen,
Risen to fly high
in the land of opportunities!"

-Vrushali

Before we get into the eradication of caste, we have to understand what caste or casteism is?

So, **Casteism** or **caste system** is processed in which people differentiate each other in a certain group or certain community with or without their interest. It is done in terms of a belief in superstition works, rituals in the name of the god.

It's the people insecurities towards his goals and ambition so that he believes that getting into a caste can create his goal or ambition easy to get, but people don't understand that by creating caste or community doesn't help you to get your goal by opposite it creates more negativity and depression which kills both goal and soul inside us.

The main culprits of casteism are we the human beings or the human mindset which creates the caste system. The people who are telling that it is created by God and we are just following that then I am sorry for those people because you really want a dire need to grow up. If it was created by God then today no one will be living happily on this earth. If caste system really matters a lot then today there will be not a country having a happy faces or else there will be not a country also there will be a casted country who rule their own caste and own people which is not possible at all. So people grow up this caste is nothing but a imagination of our mindset which rules our mind towards negativity.

Now we come to the main that is how to eradicate the caste or to stop this casteism. First of all, to stop the caste system we will work in mass so that to change the mindset of people towards these. In this modern world all are growing day by day so growing by nature or growing for ourselves shouldn't be stopped by casteism. Here as a proud citizen of India, I want to share something that today India is growing, developing and touching the heights of success in all the fields so as a responsible citizen we don't stop our success of growth by this five-letter word [*caste*]. To stop this, we have to spread love towards each people, respect there feelings and values and give equal opportunity to all so unity creates a bundle of success and growth towards ourselves and our nation also. Some of the great poets said that ***Unity is Strength***. So stop the caste and let's unite to form a better and greater nation.

Don't put a black mark of casteism towards the greenery of the motherland. Unite to hold the nation strong.
The motherland doesn't want his sons to be split out land wants to be united and fight for a good cause.

-Shaikh Sohel

No Caste No Reservation

The Caste system is another a big social evils of our country. It is one of the most destructive kinds of system which is owned and followed by our society. Even we are living in a country whose constitution is most potent in the world. But no one came forward to eradicate this caste system evils from our society. Due to the caste system, we see love like pure things gets destroy by our society. If anyone comes forward to marry in inter-caste then from their family to whole society started abusing them and started behaving abnormally.

So we just have to come together to eradicate this social evil from its roots. It is not so easy to do this but we have to change the mentality of people and our society. We should respect people not based on their caste and position but based on our humanity. We all are different in look, colour, intelligence, and status. But we all have the same spirit being Indians. In our country one slogan is very famous *"Hindu, Muslim, Sikh, Isaai, aapas me hai sb Bhai- Bhai"*. If we know all these things then why are we discriminate people on the basis of caste?

Stop reservation based on caste:

When it comes to caste then even some modern people are not ready to accept these people. When it comes in inter-caste marriage, the high caste people always discriminates lower caste people always discriminate lower caste people whether they are in a high position and they never want to marry them.

So we have to stop reservation based on caste. So that we can initiate our steps where people should treat everyone equally irrespective of their social status. For this, we have to start a campaign about caste eradication so that people can know about its adverse effects on our society.

Changing our mindset to eradicate caste word. We always see people are so much interested to know your caste and community. No matter how you look, how well educated you are but when it comes in caste, many people started discriminating them.

So to eradicate it properly first we have to change our mindset as well as our society about caste so that they know the value of everyone on the basis of status, not on caste. So that everyone gets equal status in this society.

-Anjali Jha

Abolition of the caste system

As you all know, the 21st century is the century of *FADs*. Every day a new *FAD* is coming up. But there is an all *FAD* started in 1950 which is taking the form of a long-lived fashion. Any guesses, yes it is Reservation System. It is boon for Deprived castes, but it found to be a bane for General people, as this line signifies:
Reservation made Equality but no Justice, Made general deprived and fallacious.

In this modern world, the life of deprived caste people is more enhancing and general people day by day depriving. Especially in the education system. Inadequate people are at higher posts than deserving because of reservation.

In government colleges, more students are coming from the reservation and the praiseworthy people are bound to study in less valuable colleges.

For example, this time in JEE Mains result cut off of general students is reaching skies whereas for reserved caste it is down in grounds. Here it is the exact data of cut off:-

Category	JEE Main Cut Off 2019
Common Rank List	89.7548849
Gen EWS	78.2174869
OBC NCL	74.3166557
SC	54.0128155
ST	44.3345172

You can think now that there is a reservation for GEN EWS but their cut off is not that much low as compared to other castes.

It is not easy to eradicate the caste system and reservation system but it can be made trivial in quantity. Many backward castes people don't require a reservation as they have enough necessary things to run their life but they are also exploiting it.

For this big problem, there has to be a solution, some solutions are as follows:

•There should be proper checkup of the documents of deprived castes people that they deserve it or not.

•There should befall down in the percentage reservation of them on everything.

The caste discrimination system should be stopped.

At last, let's everyone should take an oath with me that "They will never misuse their reservation power and help to stop reservation and prove that the backward caste people is no more dependent on this reservation system and they can build their life with a strong base on their own."

- Akul Agarwal

The base of Reservation Should be changed!

This system prevailed from the time of the Vedic period. During that time no one dared to change the system or went against the system. In other words, everyone accepted the fact of the caste dominating system. There were four categories of the caste ***BRAHMINS, KSHATRIYAS, VAISHYAS, SHUDRAS***. Most of the sufferers are the SUDRAS who are also known as labor class or the untouchables. They were also known as DALITS.

The reservation system was started by Dr. Bhimrao Ambedkar in the 1920'S. He started this reservation system with a positive sign with a hope that it'd help the people of India to establish themselves in the field of various opportunities. He faced various hardship to give the rights to the Dalits. He also led a satyagraha in Mahad to fight for the right of Dalits to drink water or to fetch water from the well. After giving the rights to the Dalits, he gave the regulation that this reservation system will only be held for ten years. But the people of our country still misuse it and make it mandatory for them in every aspect.

In our modern society, Almost everyone has accepted the Sudras as a vital part of this society but still in many areas they are discriminated. And the system called Reservation, which was made for them is the result of Harassment. Students aren't getting a good education because of Reserved seats everywhere. Because of the reservation system, the general category is the one who is the sufferers. In many competitive examinations such as UPSC, JEE, NEET, CLAT, AIIMS the reservation plays the game with the general category students. The SC, ST and OBC people get 15%, 7.5% and 27% quotas in respect of the general category who gets none.

As our society is accepting the changes, there should be changes in this system " Reservation" to eradicate caste system. The base of this system should be changed. People who are weak economically, they should be reserved. And then you can see the changes.

People who need the reservation are the tribal people such as santhals, gonads, etc. and the people who are below the poverty line. This kind of people should get the opportunity to use the quotas not the people who have money but don't have the ability to do something in a particular stream.

The Vedic period situation was different but in today's modern society things are different, so why the old system should be there it should be abolished. Every people should get equal opportunity, not every Brahmin are rich like the Vedic period. Equality should be given to every citizen of the country. Reservation system should be banned from our society it will give us the people who have the ability to do something and our country will also be developed like the USA and Japan.

-Akankshya Mishra

Abolishing caste-based reservation

India is a country of diverse cultures and communities which are divided. With the present context, these divisions are Caste, Religion, and Economy. These divisions form different classes which have been alienated from basic rights like education, acquisition of property, business, jobs and in some cases using public facilities like public roads or water from a public place. In order to compensate for the mistreatment of those classes, the reservation was introduced. But today it has been exploited by privileged people of society and the underprivileged remain disregarded. It was implemented so that the backward classes could get their rights, division of classes will be minimized and equality shall prevail. But in reality, privileges for backward classes have induced envy in other classes of the society, resulting in demand for similar privileges for themselves. The latest example of which is Maratha Reservation in Maharashtra after which the reserved quota for the state reached 74% (maximum limit is 50% as per constitution). Thus the present reservation system has failed miserably and indeed has added fuel to the fire.

No doubt that society has also failed in its responsibility to treat every individual equally irrespective of class. If the motive was equal opportunity to every backward

class, then the efforts should have been made in empowering backward classes before they enter into competing with other classes of the society. But there was a negligible effort made in this field.
By abolishing the present reservation system, we can replace it by *Socio-Economic reservation.*

20% on the economic basis for economically weak candidates regardless of caste or tribe.

20% for socially and educationally weak candidates using interdisciplinary review can identify deserving candidates by using different factors like:

1. first-generation students (Zero educational background).

2. single parent-child.

3. educated from a remote/rural area.

4. physically challenged/medically dependent.

5. socially deprived of fundamental rights.

6. orphan/homeless.

7. tragic family history/background.

8. educationally weak family background.

9. strong exclusive education or extra-ordinary performance in the main subject but a low score in other extraneous subjects. and more.

Additionally, the Government can provide financial support to encourage socially weak sections of society by providing them free counseling, tuitions, books, etc. But there is a possibility of a creamy layer or already privileged people taking advantage of this by doctoring information. This can be dealt with severe punishment like expulsion, imprisonment and financial penalty for falsifying information and misusing government facilities for self-interest.

The somewhat similar system acts in 8 states of USA, they have abolished their old race-based affirmative action and introduced A similar system. It resulted in an increase in a number of deserving backward class candidates.

It's also true that a fixed quota on the basis of these factors doesn't guarantee that it won't leave any deserving candidate unconsidered. But till the society becomes uniform and people become self-sufficient, such system should function.

So we need a reform which can encourage underprivileged sections of society irrespective of caste. At the same time, we have to start treating everyone equally. Can we do it?

-Aakash Karanjavkar

Reduction of different castes of all religions and to make unique caste in education!

As we know that today in India, more than 41% of people are from lower caste ones and they are getting places in IIT for fewer marks even higher caste one struggled by hard of high scores.

Drawbacks for higher caste in Education:

The lower caste ones are employed in MNC companies, but higher caste ones are being affected by them because of reservation.

In the constitution, it is there that the one who is SC, ST, BC candidates are considered as lower caste people. The OC candidates are higher caste ones. In previous years, they consider that lower caste people are economically weak to educate their children so they neglect their children's education. To eradicate this, Dr. Ambedkar introduced reservation based on caste to have education for all classes of people but this became a drawback for merit students in a higher caste. They are not capable to get seats in good colleges but even they are poor but the lower caste ones even rich getting places in a good college with low marks.

Reasons for this problem:

As we know that still today India is facing drawbacks in education and even it can't balance the poor and rich to educate all sectors of people. Actually, the fault is in our constitution as there is an amendment if we can control our generations we can change the rules as per the updation of people lifestyles, but it was showing a huge impact on the education sector. Education is only a Bane for rich and lower caste but it became a boon for high caste and low economy background without public awareness people of the lower economy who can't able to study are getting placed in mills, mines, as child labors who are killing their golden life. And parents too who are not educated spoiling their children's life. Women are also being affected by this economy. The lower caste with no economy is being affected and getting married at a lower age who are killing their lives for their parents. As per California University, 67% in today India is facing this problem, women below 18 are also getting married to high aged boys for money so if it continues we should pay huge consequences on this involvement.

Ways to eradicate this problem:

1. By removing the qualifying marks based on caste 2. By implementation of allotting seats based on merit wise

3. By providing reservation only for the economy, not for caste.

Reduction of Caste System:

The caste discrimination in India is due to our diversion of castes as a survey there are 5000 castes in India if we continue this constitution we can be back in education, development, etc. This can be reduced by marking all religions in India as one caste, and there will be no reservations based on caste then our India can become free from caste discrimination. But this will be difficult to proceed to annex this method we should conduct rallies, strikes, public meetings for awareness, and by announcing ads in media, paper, internet blogs, social media to highlight this idea.

If we reduce all castes and form one caste called Humanism, it will be helpful for our new generations.

- Ch. Mahesh Babu

Narrow Mindedness of People

How much the person has progressed in every field today, but his narrow Mindedness still exists, and his thinking is confined to the small and big Caste drop. Because Man makes things great, but when it comes to something, he starts talking loudly and low, and that is the main reason why casteism is still rampant or is not ending because of the very small thoughts of society. Secondly, unemployment is also the main reason for the rise of casteism somewhere the government is also supportive in increasing this section because reservation is a term that promotes casteism and makes humans think that we belong to general category so we didn't get the profit, those who are in Scheduled tribes (ST) may get the benefit. So it is absolutely wrong because the educated people should have equal right, in the education systems, whether it is a general or a reserved category but today this reservation has caused so much distress that the younger generation even being educated is suffering from unemployment, the government should eliminate this demon of reservation because it is killing everybody, whether it is small or tall and degrading.

Thirdly, making of different caste communities, one of the thinking of man here is that he does big things when it comes to raising the stuff, he lags behind and that is why the distinction of caste is still intact. Different groups are being made, Punjabis, Brahmin, etc. The feeling of alienation in different groups is that the people of the downhole cannot have any community; they cannot exist. But the rule should say that together is equal and should have equal rights.

Now if we talk about how to eradicate or solve this, then Human should eliminate their narrow ideology. Eliminate the demon of the reservation should be abolished completely. No part should be done in any of the department everybody should be treated all together festival of Muslim, Sikh or Hindu any of the religion should be celebrated at one place, altogether. The general category and scheduled tribe should have the administrative educationally equal rights so that no youth is unemployed as Unemployment is also the main reason for the crime line.

We should aware people about raising their voice for wrong because that's how the world goes.

- Shrangarika Sharma

In most of the developing countries, "Caste" is a word which describes people intelligence, manner, culture in fact whole humanity and India is one of them. No one wants to get discriminated by their caste. Whatever the consequences were, for making caste system but if it is not going in favor of every person then this system should be stopped and for that person should be educated, well aware, self-confident and most importantly they should change their mentality. I always wonder every human has the same blood same morphology then why this discrimination?

One of the reason to eradicate this caste system is **"Politics of Caste"**, every leader which belongs to a particular community is going to support their community more than others so that thing makes discrimination and also they promote one thing that people of their community well embrace because those leaders know they have "vote bank" from that community and ultimately the wrong leader rise up because of this, which not only prove himself a wrong leader but also prove himself a wrong leader for nation.

We should spread love and positivity because ***"Caste is a curse which embraces the worse"***.

India is a democratic country but when it comes in terms of caste and religion the whole democracy is besieged by culture and orthodox mentality.

My question to those people who support caste system is that whenever the caste and religion come people start taking advantage of their reservation but if someone points out them by their caste then why it becomes offensive. The reservation itself is proof that our country still needs "crutches" and how a country can grow by moving on crutches. In my opinion "if only poverty alleviation program" will implement completely rather than "caste-based reservation" so that would be a more convenient way to eradicate this caste system.

"Caste is the cluster if It is not removed now, so it will become a tumor later".

- Sourav Rathour

As we already know, in India the untouchables or we can say 'Dalits' had always been discriminated as they belonged to a lower caste. In the previous era, they were deprived of so many rights, education and freedom of occupation. Also, they were subjected to stigmatized manual labor or slavery. They were also segregated from other citizens. But after some time, as a result of their revolt against their discrimination, they had been given some rights of getting proper education, jobs, and other facilities. Yet they are not treated equally as other people are. They are still biased on the basis of a number of aspects. To abolish this caste system I think we should first focus on social and economic equality of Dalits.

Equality in Social and Economical Aspects:

At present, the political parties are mainly constituted on the basis of caste or religion. They primarily work for the welfare of their class group. Substantially, they make efforts to encourage their social class.

• This should be prohibited. I think each political party must be constituted in such a way that every part have at least one or two members belonging to lower castes. So as to provide equal social rights to the people of each caste.

• They should be permitted to enjoy the same rights as others.

• There should be a community that makes sure that no one is trying to criticize any caste or religion in any manner.

• In view of the fact that discrimination of such people leads to unemployment and hence poverty. Consequently, an adequate number of job opportunities should be provided in order to maintain economic equality.

Dividing people due to their lower castes will make people more rebellious. Hence, we should suppress the process of casteism. We can conclude that one of the main reason for poverty is an economical imbalance of such caste groups, so equality in this aspect will undoubtedly lead to abolish poverty. Giving them equal opportunities to participate in the basic, economic, and social functioning of the society, they will also contribute to the development of our country.

-Naina Mishra

Culture of India is the best culture in the world. It teaches us a lesson of brotherhood. Our family system is guiding all the societies of this Universe. We live together and understand each other.

As the caste system, I am surprised why our forefathers had adopted this system. Educated and Modern society does not follow this system. This is a good sign of our modern society. But this is very ridiculous that some of us are making differences on the basis of castes in society. All of us know very well that creator of all is a supreme power, GOD. Our constitution gives us equal rights, not discrimination. Nowadays, the caste system is disappearing day-by-day, because all people of modern society are adopting the same occupations, professions, and businesses. People from all caste are becoming Doctors, Engineers, CAs, Administrators, etc.

In ancient India, people made castes on the basis of their works. Successors were adopting their parental professions. Group of persons doing the same work were recognized by caste. But today's scenario has totally changed. We can see that children aren't doing the same job as their parents.

So, in this position, the caste system has no meaning. As it creates discrimination and separates all of us from each other, it must be removed from our system and thoughts also. If we want to make our country advance and world leader, we must give up this system for the sake of our country. Otherwise, it will divide us into groups which will be dangerous.

Let's make a promise to give it up totally and make our country strong.

49

-Satbir Singh Patel

Casteism is eradicating our society from every way!

Caste is a man-made system of a social ladder which cannot be avoided in the Indian culture. Caste-based criticism is very much in practice & due to this cases like loss of lives is common to be all.

Let's see some ways to defend:-

Education:

We all know that in every institution there is at least 30% of seats are reserved for backward classes. We all feel every people from these backward classes needs opportunity. There are many students from good financial background take this as an advantage and this should be changed and the institutions can change this and focus on the financial background of students for reserving seats.

Society:

This is the biggest factor. Still, now we all have the practice of dowry, segregation of people those who are from a lower caste, following superstitions. For this reason, we really need to change our mentality our ideology and of course the way of our thinking that a human being is born with the particular identity of own not any religious identity.

Lastly, Raise your voice against any kind of discrimination. Remember, one voice can change everything and will help us to live a decent life.

- Sulagna Chakraborty

Casteism Annihilation at Educational Level

To my mind, Casteism takes its root at education itself. Annihilation of Casteism from education will prove panacea to society. As it is one of the prevalent social disasters in the world. Owing to which, communal riots and sectarian violence takes place most of the time. As a result, society is having its dehumanized face in front of us.

It is the Irony of humans' life that when a person takes birth, he is brought up with no discrimination in terms of caste and class. As they begin their journey with their education, they are made to realize the caste they belong to whether General, OBC or SC/ST. Here, the real casteism starts and then people's mindset comes with a difference. It affects their mind completely that make them behave discriminatingly. Whether how much educated they are, the circumstances in which they grow affects them the most. And thus casteism continues to come in practice wherein the segregation of humanity starts in terms of caste and class.

Therefore, there should be caste free education without categorization of humanity. People should know human as human, not as caste or class. Then the people will have neither the print of casteism in their mind nor it is in their practice.

So, the change is to be brought in the education system itself where in human can expects humanity from one another not the segregation of it. As it is the place, wherein if the changes are brought, it will create a healthy society with no difference. Inter-caste marriage is considered to be the best suitable example to annihilate casteism from our society. And it is still evident in our society. And it truly proved healthy in most of the cases. Though, if caste categorization is removed from the education system, it can also set another best example for caste categorization abolishment. And it can be one of the solutions too, to Annihilate casteism from our society permanently.

-Sweta Kumari

Caste, a word normal to read but painful when applied. From time immemorable, the system of division of human based on caste has been prevailing in our society. This leads to division and partiality among us, among humans! Beneath the skin and muscle folds, we are alike. We all have 206 bones. We are same because we have been created in the same way. But the system of caste division has been created by us and this leads to inhuman activities among these similar beings.

The wound by a knife can heal but not the wound by tongue. And just imagine the mental brutality felt by a so called "*untouchable*" when he is called so or treated like.

This system of caste must be entirely removed from our society for a healthy generation of us and a generation to come. The root cause of all these lies in one word "Education". And yes, education is the fundamental cure by which this system can be removed.

This system started at a time when the level of education was negligible and therefore was more prevalent. As we are progressing in education, we, as on today, are at least thinking of this as an issue to be talked about and taken seriously. Therefore educating the young generation and removing the concept of caste from their root can lead to a caste free healthy society. Others include letting children mingle with everyone in the society and being friends, holding get-togethers and functions, cultural ceremonies in the society where everyone can take active part and live like one, human being!

55

-Hafizur Rahman

In this world of the 21st century, many problems are being faced from which "CASTE SYSTEM" is one of the most serious problems.

If we talk about the caste system it is one of the ancient problems. In ancient times, people use to discriminate in education according to their caste. According to them if a father is a doctor, then the son will also study for the doctor and no other knowledge will be provided to him/her.

We live in "MORDEN WORLD" where people can do anything to maintain their status, protect the reputation of their family. People have become so orthodox that still at some parts of our country or we can say some villages "***HONOR KILLING***" is being practiced which have taken the lives of many innocent.

We see sweepers, gardner, drivers, watchman, maid, etc. who plays a major role in our day to life but no respect is given to them just because they are from the lower cast! They too are humans and deserve the same respect as we give to the high caste people. They should not be kept aside.

As we saw caste discrimination has become the major problem but how to end this ?

To end this, parents have to stop controlling their children's mind. They should stop taking their decision. In fact, parents should teach their children that every person should be judged by his/her heart and not by face or caste. We should give our child knowledge of love between the people, not only bookish knowledge, we should teach them to think from their heart and not the brain. This will change their thinking and that will be a huge step to end this system.

Next, we should change our education system which keeps the children away from getting all kind of knowledge. Like ancient times we shouldn't spread negative thinking. All should be together without thinking of any caste, color or sex. The Government has already taken step forward of removing this caste system by developing various programs and they are developing very fast.
The honor killing which had been declared illegal by the government, and which is still in the act should be stopped immediately. The youth should raise their voice to stop all this. "***Every big thing starts with a small step***".

We say that we have become modern but the thing is we have become modern only by our looks and behavior and not by our mind. The very first thing we should learn and even teach our children's is to become modern by our mind.

So, before saying yourself modern try to remove negative thinking from your mind and you, yourself can see a change in the world and a better way of living.

Let our children's see the world with their own eyes.
Let not force them to do things of our choice.

58

-Harsh Bhadoriya

Education paves the way

When you look back to your early years when you were a child, did it ever happened to you that you didn't talk to someone because they had a different name, a varied color or creed? You wouldn't even have had known what that means. We're not born with differences in our mind. We absorb them. We're fed by the people all around, the grown-up people, the wise people.

Children's brains are like molds. If they're fed with the right morals, they'll absorb good things and their consciousness will filter out the rest. Probably the best way to counter casteism is to feed children that there is no casteism. We cannot abolish it in overnight, waking up the next morning in the world free if caste. People just won't give up because that's what they've believed in all their lives. The division is a humanitarian nature. We've evolved that way. Nations, languages, creeds. Divisions are either based on beliefs or on choices we weren't offered. No division is ever harmful unless we begin to differentiate amongst divisions.

Making people feel more or less. Trying to equalize society by uplifting personal motives. Suppressing a few sections and projecting a few making people fight one another in a race of achieving some form of glory for a particular section of society.

We call them divisions but these divisions do bind people through a common belief. The divisions will forever exist because not everyone can have the same beliefs. But we're not in a time where just a name should make you more or less. It should just be your identity, nothing more and nothing less.

One of the preventive steps that could be taken is to provide education to children to respect individuals over caste, by providing them caste-based education or a subject related to it. Not only the children but their parents should also be taught about equality so that they can nurture their children when they're not at school and from the beginning of their lives. It is important to take such steps as India is a young country with over 50% population in the age group of 20-35. Though these steps look slow but will have a wider range and a long term impact for the development of each individual of this country.

If someday with all the knowledge we possess and the observations we've made, we could provide our children with enough values that they could in no time say that these differences are not worth it. If we could feed them with values that would help their eyes not to filter anyone on the basis of his identity, only then we'll have a peaceful society.

-Apurv Bhardwaj

Remove the wrong idea of caste

Older people, like those in the age group of our parents or grandparents, believe in the caste system much more compared to us. Forget about inter-caste marriages or such kind of love affairs, many of them don't even support the friendship of their children, with children from another caste. What can we do?

1. One simple solution is to introduce them to people from other (lower) castes, like, we can introduce our parents to our friends, without revealing the actual caste of friends. Let them come closer and let the parents build their trust in their friends and then we can reveal that they belong to some other caste. This may prove to be a bit shocking for the parents, but they will eventually realize that people from other caste are not as bad as they thought them to be.

2. The other thing that can be done is, we can ask those friends to help us in some of our worst problems, and let this be known to our families, that, 'one particular friend of mine, who belongs to some other (lower) caste is helping me, when my family is in need. In both these ways, our families will develop a positive image regarding people from different (lower) castes, and if these steps are followed on large scale, this will help in eradicating the problem of the caste system.

The caste system was originally formed with good intention, so that, all the people can know their responsibility and their importance in society. But, later on, it turned out to be one of the biggest evils of the society. The lower caste people were shown no mercy and were deprived of the basic necessities, forget any facilities. They were made to live like slaves. They were not supposed to enter the temples, as it was thought by the upper caste people, that, this was the insult of God. Presently, many laws have been passed by the government, so that, the lower caste people can get the rights, which they deserve being the citizens of India. Even, people are getting conscious about this topic. People have started to realize the injustice, that the people of lower castes go through.

But, until and unless all of us try on our own, this problem cannot be fully removed. And, it would be much better, if instead of trying it out on the extreme levels, like inter-caste marriage, etc., we try to take smaller steps, like changing the thinking of the society, by trying to change the thinking of our families (by the above-mentioned ways). This would be a slow step, but, if we show consistency, then it can help us bring about a large change in the society.

-Udisha Singh

"Democracy is not simply a license to indulge individual whims and proclivities. It is also holding oneself accountable to some reasonable degree for the conditions of peace and chaos that impact the lives of those who inhabit one's beloved extended community."

-Aberjhani

In a democratic country like India, it becomes necessary for both the citizens as well as the politicians and government to change their attitude. We are now hardly left with any time to make policies, now it's time to implement them. Following are some areas which I would like to highlight:

Caste community/Organization based on castes:

These kind of organizations are most prevalent in small towns and villages, although even the cities aren't completely out of the game. The goals of these organizations vary, but discrimination is common. They take into account the problems and solutions of people of a single kind of community only, which leads to the suffering of the others. Such organizations must be banned, whether registered or unregistered.

Matrimonial advertisements/sites:

The matrimonial ads in the newspapers, or in the matrimonial sites are divided on the basis of caste. This weighs the caste of the candidate heavier than the qualities that a person possess. The government has the ultimate power to end this and change the complete structure.

Inter-caste marriages:

Such marriages should be encouraged by the family, relatives, fellows, friends, civilians, and the government. Now many people will argue that what's the government's role in it. In a country with a continuously growing population like India, the government can easily do it by providing incentives, probably by offering a loan to the new couple for building a house, etc.

Temple priests:

In India, the religious beliefs and practices of the people are top-notch, as well as quite conservative, possessive and discriminatory. Here the "untouchables" or the people of lower castes are allowed to sit in front of the religious institutions to beg but are strictly not allowed to even come inside them. In such a condition, it sounds uncanny to say that such people should be made the priests, but it also sounds quite necessary and on point. This will be a major transformation in the current scenario, although only the government has the power to make it a strict law which is to be followed by all.

As mentioned initially, I feel the entire problems roots to people's mentality and their attitude towards a particular issue. It is rightly said that we won't be realizing the pain of

others unless we are put up in the same situation. We should try to realize the significance of coexistence. Blaming or ignoring won't solve the purpose. It's time when we should start "being human"!

-Anisha Garg

Caste system in India is very unique considering it's a culturally diverse country. We can eradicate the caste system by slowly encouraging people to be more flexible with their thoughts. They have become so in recent times and also continue to do so. But the caste system has been in India for a very long time and totally eradicating them will take a large amount of time and patience. But it is not impossible to do so and we can adopt a few measures to build the stepping stones to build that path.

1. We can encourage people to not judge someone by their Jat and Varna and for that, we need to be more liberal in promoting equality in schools.

2. We can also ask for the government's aid by asking them to slowly dissolve the castes in time.

3. The government should also remove the reservation policy which deepens the division along caste lines and should extend help by financially supporting people based on their financial background.

We need to understand that we should destroy this caste system before it destroys us in the future. The caste system was created by the British Raj as a divide and rule policy. Though the constitution abolished it, the problem of untouchability still remains in rural areas.

-Ritika Dasgupta

Caste and Eradication of Caste

'Caste' is only a word to tell the difference between living being, not for a human being. For example difference in animals, birds, insects, reptiles, etc. Buffalo is a specific caste of the animal. Other animals are quite different than other animals. A cow is different, an ox is different, horse, monkey, donkey, lion, tiger, dog, elephant all are different. Such as crow is different than other birds, sparrow, eagle, kite, dove, etc. All birds are quite different. Same reptiles and insects etc. are. It can be good for animals because they don't study, they don't know values, they don't have thinking power as human beings. But how can we imagine it for human beings? It's beyond my understanding. But it is being used and adopted by some mentally ill but clever people for their personal benefits. This casteism is not to tell specializations of the human being but to miss use of their mind for the specific self of the people who want to rule over common and simple people. This is the policy of 'Divide and Rule '. It is the technique to empower the sovereign to control subjects, population, or fraction of different interest who collectively might be able to oppose his rule. It's happening with the innocent people of our country what we know well but do not want to oppose to get rid of being the prey of sovereigns. The traditional, orthodox, selfish people, social evils and politicians offer poison through intrigue to every Indian since their childhood. Some people are elated because they are considered from higher caste (savarnas). But some people consider them oppressor. The people think that they enjoy that kind of highness. But I totally oppose it because they are also prisoners of hatred. They are not free from unanalyzed jealousy. No one takes birth with jealousy. They have learned it through mentally sick people in the society which is against humanism.

The people who belong to lower caste. They are mentally demoralized because they are considered from a low caste which doesn't let them be confident. They think that the people of higher caste oppress them so they have an ill feeling for them even if they have to work under their orders or instructions. The stigma of casteism doesn't let generate initial fraternity and equality among the people which is also the main reason to deplete integration and the good feeling among our countrymen. In both of the notions, the people of higher castes and lower castes are being crushed, one from hatred and another one from oppression which is incorrigible disease and its against the rule of supreme power whatever it is called God, Allah Ishwar, etc.

But the cure for that kind of disease is ERADICATION OF CASTE

It has become very essential for us to eradicate the casteism form our society because it teaches animalism which is very hazardous for human being and humanity. Both things are necessary not only for the people of India but also for the world. Being democratic people of India we have the right to oppose such people who reign on us and have responsibility for the solution of our every problem. But it is the profound pain that they use our mind and we the people let them use, wow! How smart we are. It's a shame on us that we let it be done. Why we the people do not raise our voice against casteism? Why we are mentally weak? Why? I would like to enlighten the simple way **to eradicate casteism if govt. of our country should make a law that writing alias and title after the name is a crime and people who do such will have to go to jail for five years and mental hospital for three years. The people who are habitual to add title and alias after their names. They should add their qualification or profession after their name** e.g. Aneesh MBBS Doctor, Manoj ASI, Deepak Advocate, Vijay MLA, Rajesh Farmer, etc. that will generate curiosity among people to be higher and to get higher education or post. This will be more beneficial for our country.

For this, we need to nationalize education so that everybody will have an equal opportunity to prove themselves. This will remove educational reservation and caste-based reservation. It will leave only economical reservation which should be the highest _interest of every govt. to survive in the world. Then there would be only one struggle to economize the people which would be the best interest for our country._

Caste will be eradicated and people will be able to get eligible life partner and society will be quality-based, not caste-based. Specially I want to ask people who believe in God. Does He generate a person in caste? Yes, He does it as male, female and eunuch not more than that. He does only this, why are they misguided by so-called agents of God. You should believe in God or in the agents of God? Don't you have your own mind? Just think over it. I know dear readers that some evil-minded who don't like equality will oppose my this thought but let them do. I will always write and do against blind faith and unfair because I thought with my own mind, I am neither theist nor atheist, I am realistic. I am writing this article who really love peace and fraternity so they will definitely response it positively. Yet I invite criticizer on this article. They can send their response by mail to mlbsamrath1@gmail.com

-Madan English Lecturer

Castes in India represent the hierarchical system that was created in the Vedic era in order to designate people on the basis of the kind of work they chose to do. It was only in the Later Vedic Era that the caste system became so stringent. The caste of the child was pre-decided, the hereditary devolution of caste and hence the status associated with it became a norm. The modern caste system is a reminiscence of the same old caste system that has resulted in the stratification of the classes, where people at the bottom of this hierarchy have to suffer the most. It is heart-rending and tragic to know that there is a certain section of people who despite being in the 21st century are still caught up in the clutches of this age-old, obsolete system that was supposed to be abolished centuries ago.

URBANISATION:

Many ideas come to my mind when I think of how to detach this inextricably woven thread of caste from the fabric of our society. I think of reservation, inter-caste marriages, punitive actions for caste bullies, but all these have led to nothing but disappointment since these ways cannot be used to achieve an ideal society where no one cares what the other person's caste is like they do in cities. So my silver bullet solution to this evil of caste system is Urbanisation.

Lesser opportunities mean lower self-confidence which is one of the main reason that people succumb to these primitive norms that are catastrophic to their self-respect but with opportunities comes confidence and in cities, there are many such opportunities to grasp. Higher or vocational education, in fact, is a far fetched dream for some poor family living in the village belonging even to the upper castes leave alone the poor people of lower strata who are already a victim of both dearth of money and stigmas of society. The kind of exposure and plethora of opportunities in cities are enormous. In addition to that due to the higher level of education among the people of towns and cities not many practices the caste system with much rigidity.

Cities, in fact, are a hub of economical advantage that provides wealth, employment and quality of life to the table. They promote social transformation. The fact that life in cities is extremely busy that nobody actually has got time to spare into such a menial job of caste bullying. With exposure comes awareness too so if somebody in a city is bullied or harassed because of his caste he will be more aware of his rights and hence more capable to take action than someone who is similarly placed but in a village.

This process of urbanization is not free from pitfalls due to a limited number of opportunities, failure to grasp which might lead to further alienation. But since we have many laws in place and education coupled with reservation in an urban society will prove to be a silver bullet solution to this deeply rooted fungus of the caste system.

Urbanization undermines caste. Caste is not a matter of concern in cities as much it is in rural areas. This relative anonymity of caste in an urban area makes urbanization an impeccable panacea for the caste system. The increase in the rate of urbanization with time will surely put an end to this age-old disease of the caste system that has crippled our society.

-Harshita Sevaldasani

Extirpation of the caste system through an annihilation gun of education and human psychology!

Our present society is the perfect example of an oxymoron. At the present time, when we are trying to walk through the progressive, liberal and modern path, science and technology is approaching the zenith of success then a part of society still discriminate people on the ground of caste. The lower class is still oppressed by the higher class. So the question arises how the words lower class and upper class exist in the progressive world? Is the modern world a vizard of regressive society which is actually walking behind? what is the solution?

To discuss the topic we shall first talk about the creation of caste. In the Indian context, we can say that the caste system was introduced during the Vedic period. Dravidians are the oldest residents of India. Aryans came from middle Asia (though there is controversy this is the most popular theory). And Basically, It was created on the ground of occupation. Racism was also a factor. So actually the caste system was simply a classification of the society. But the problem is when there exists discrimination for this classification. And a class of society started to dominate over the others. So a part of the society was deprived of all the benefits.

This scenario evoluted over time. But the basic system of caste and the idea of discrimination, untouchability remain unchanged. In the post-Independent time, the government also tried to eradicate the caste system. The constitution of India also tells us not to discriminate people on the ground of caste (article 15). It also prohibits untouchability (article 17). Still, the picture has not changed yet.

From all the previous discussions we can say that the basic idea of the caste system has a permanent place in our psychology. We can bring an example. Think about a middle-class housewife who is watching a movie where the hero loves the heroine. But the basic problem in their relationship is either their economical background difference or the caste. In that case, that housewife will support their relationship. But in real life, she will not! There are some common solutions like inter-caste marriage, exclusion of surname and introduction of common surname, etc. We may raise questions on reservation system also. But here we shall think from the different reference frame.

A part of the society strongly believes in religious instructions. What is religion? If we read the literature of the different religions we can say, all the religions are actually philosophy, which binds the group of people through some rules and regulations and gives instructions for regulated life. But they were relevant when the religion was created. Time has changed. The character of human, lifestyle has also changed. But the rules are the same. The caste system is part of religious thought. So if we amend the regressive ideas of religion, we may eradicate the caste system from the root. But clearly, this is not an easy way because public sentiment is associated with this. Here the basic problem is the government can not interfere directly in this ground. But we have seen in 1956 the Hindu Marriage Act legalized inter-caste marriage. In recent times, we have also seen that the government has prohibited the triple talaq system. It means if the religious instructions are against the human government interferes. The caste system is also an idea against "Unification". The idea of unification is associated with nationalism. So why the government can't think about the amendment of nasty rules where people are categorized?

Behind every problem of society, a common cause is the lack of education. The idea of caste should be destroyed at the stage of infancy. From the beginning of education inclusion of the subject social science should introduce. So that the child psychology will grow up in a progressive way. Awareness is a wcapon also. We often see the advertisement for awareness. Eradication of caste may be the subject of advertisement also. Tv, radio social media are strong weapons in this time. The government should organize different Campaigns, especially in the village areas. Introduction of some strong laws in case of persecutions is also necessary.

But above all both, the government and people should have a positive approach.

The problem is the government is politically motivated and political parties use the different part of the society for the self-interest. A recent web series LEILA has shown the churlish future where the caste systems, classification of the society are in the extreme form. We can not tell this just an imaginary story of future rather an eutopia for a bigot.

Should not we think about this problem seriously? Are we actually looking forward or just making some discussions only in some magazine and in TV program? Are we inviting a dystopian world?

-Soumick Mukherjee

Hinduism is not a religion but an Ideology

For thousands of years people have been discriminating each other following the ideas that they thought to be made by the gods, but the reality is these systems were not made by god but these were prevailed and misinterpreted by the people who wanted to rule by dividing the people so that they can never protest against them.

The religious scriptures and books never taught us to discriminate. Instead, they always focused on one thing i.e., to perceive each other not as superior or inferior but as humans. They mainly focused on the nature and deeds of the person rather than the caste he belongs to. In ancient times, some wise men put people in various groups such as *Brahmin, Kshatriya, Vaishya & Dalit,* these groups were not made to put a tag of inferior or superior but their groups were made to provide specific works to people and to run the society in a systematic and orderly manner but in the ravages of time people for their own agenda started to further divide and put a tag of inferior and superior.

These concepts of untouchability have prevailed but the people who only wanted others to work under them and slowly the groups made for the welfare of the society turned out to be the biggest curse on it.

The biggest reason, people believe in the caste system is because their mind is filled with lies that these were made by the gods and that's the only reason because of which this curse still exists. India has an image of a land of different religions. A place where different religions rest on the same land for centuries, here people would do anything for their religion and follow it blindly without assuring it's righteousness.

The best way to erase a problem is to destroy its roots, we have to look from where it started. People need to be taught and acknowledged about the reasons why these caste systems were made and how the thing that was meant to be betterment turned out to be a curse. They need to be acknowledged about the true history of the caste system.
The people in India only understand the language of religion and that's where the solution to this curse exists.

People can be acknowledged by the tales from Ramayana and Mahabharata.

For example: How Lord Rama ate the berries from the hands of a lower caste Sabri and how Lord Krishna asked a lower caste to put sandalwood in his forehead.

These tales clearly indicate and tell us that how even their gods were against this curse.

People can be acknowledged by these tales by making posters for telling these stories, or even a drama or a play can be organized based on these tales. These tales will clearly tell people that even Lord Rama, the one we worship didn't believe in this curse so why we are dividing humans for our own uses. There are various incidents in this modern world where some famous personalities themselves opposed it.

Again the solution to a problem lies in its roots, so if people understand the language of religion they should be taught in the same language. They should be acknowledged and told about these tales and asked to learn from it for the betterment of the country and the society.

-Kaushik Singh Maravi

Indian society is divided into various sects and classes. This is because of the caste system which is prevalent in the country. The roots of the caste system go back to the ancient Vedas dividing people on the basis of varna or occupation. It has brought many evils in society. Our government is constantly trying to curb the chronic problems related to this diseased ritual & elevate the true equality among the people of our country. The caste system which has divided our society into different sectorial classes & groups is playing a predominant role in our society despite adequate growth of culture & civilization. The terms "*Scheduled Caste or Scheduled Tribe*" (SC/ST) are the official terms used by the government to categorize the people under 'untouchables', tribes & lower classes. The roots of the caste system are glorifying observed since ancient ages, while one view discriminates between the castes as upper and lower castes on the basis of their origin, another view traces the origin of the castes to varnas which classifies the caste system on the basis of their functions. Since then, it was found that undue advantage was taken by the section of people having an upper hand and a say in the community, leading to discrimination and exploitation of the weaker sections of the community. Some dangerous sides of this caste system are the following:

In India, there are many villages which are living in the beliefs of mass dividation on the basis of caste, classes & creeds. They are incessantly following the bullshit rules like the lower class people can't use the same water from the same wells which the upper classes are using or, drawing lines between their stay.

Sometimes people from lower class or 'Dalits' can't access to the better facilities of electricity or sanitation or water pumps from neighborhoods whereas upper classes consume the betterment of electricity, sanitation or waterlines. Lower class people are literally deprived of better education, medical facility or housing whereas the upper class takes all the advantages.

'Dalits' are trampled of from doing respectable jobs as they are restricted to some occupations like sanitation work, plantation work, leather works, cleaning streets, etc.

They are subjected to exploitation in the name of debt, tradition, etc., to work as laborers or perform menial tasks for generations together.

Gender-based violence is common among the people belonging from the lower class. Often, the woman from the lower class is seen suffering from sexual assault, mob lynching, allegations of 'Dyaan' tags, etc. which are however not acceptable anyway.

Though the government has enacted several laws to protect these weaker class of society, it hasn't shown any effectiveness in their regular life. One thing to be noticed that, if these people are facing problems from all spheres of life, there are still many taking the fruits of the laws enacted to save them just for the sake of our damaged administration. The advantage-takers who are consuming dependencies are the following:

Having an adequate amount of wealth & access to the betterment of primary needs, some clever lower classes still take the facility of their SC/ST quota whereas a needy general commoner can't avail such facilities as the high rate of expenses. People from lower class, creed or SC/ST are observed to take the advantages of better facility in case of education in spite of scoring low or taking the scholarships with a minimum of 45-50% score in any competitive exams or board exams & with a placement of high ranked school or colleges whereas people from general category securing proper scores or more than 80% face deprivation to avail educational institution for their quality. Then comes the "Cut-off" thing in every competitive exam or medical, engineering entrance of govt. Jobs where the cut-off marks usually range very low for the reserved people & range sky-high for the unreserved people. So, they easily get entered with scoring a little & general categorized are deprived to gather their seats on the basis of their merit. Unemployment is high on our country & then several rules are saving those so-called reserved & people out of this secure zone are crying for placement & suffering from inferiority complexes, depression & severe mental unhealthiness. The suicide rates have touched the huge figure of around 45,000 or 46,000 per year for the mass unemployment, that is causing an alarming situation today.

So, there are so many reasons why we shouldn't anymore bear the curse of caste system & regularize it in our daily life. Our main aim should be to create a society free of caste, creed, religion & social discrimination. We should look after the issues of racism, abolition of untouchability, abolition of reservation system in means of public access, govt. jobs, school, colleges or private sectors etc., elimination of social discrimination in basis of caste-religion or varnas, establishment of complete right to equality for each citizen of our country & justice to the roles of humanity. This is our country, our society & our very own civilization, & to protect them from all the evil spirit, it is our responsibility to maintain sovereignty & bring reformation to the ancient stigmas & stereotypes. After all, we are the pathfinders of the new revolution of our country & we should definitely work on this to recreate a healthy & wealthy society providing equality in all spheres of life.

-Suchismita Ghoshal

The caste system has been prevailing in India for a very long time. I have been observing it in many stages of my life in many scenarios like discrimination, honor killing, disapproval of inter-caste marriages and many more. Of all the above, the worst experience that I had with respect to the Caste System is the influence it has on movies. I come from a place called Guntur in Andhra Pradesh. I am a movie maniac and I love everything about movies, starting from fixing a plot, writing a story, bringing it on screen and finally reviewing it. I was deeply disappointed when the fate of a film is decided by the caste of the hero. I really don't understand the concept that if you belong to a particular caste, you should encourage and appreciate only that particular hero and discriminate remaining all other actors. What amazes me more is the previous generation starts cultivating the seeds that this is supposed to be this way. I was flabbergasted when one of my colleague at the office asked my caste and commented that why are you supporting that hero when you are not supposed to. Her parents asked her to support only the actors that are their caste and that's how she was brought up and can you imagine that she is from Chennai and she was talking about Telugu film Industry. The best way to solve this is to deal from the roots. If the leads of opposing caste of the current existing old generation come together for a multi-starrer, a lot of people would actually start understanding the actual essence. The name and caste of the actors should not be revealed or at least not publicly elevated or exhibited. It starts with one family and spreads to a long chain of the family with in-laws and successors of the families turning to be to become actors. The problem is with people whose opinion or perspective can never be changed just like that. So decreasing the importance of caste and promoting multi-starrer movies with opposite caste could actually bring some change on a positive note. The actors bonding with other co-actors irrespective of their caste and elevating the bond on social media also could be one major breakthrough in bringing a change in the mindset of the audience.

-Tejaswi Vajinepalli

One Soul One God

It's the 21st Century, people have moved to Mars and Moon, technology has evolved so much, people have become smarter and gadgets have gone way ahead. The world is changing so rapidly but there is something which has not changed-mind set of people especially in South East Asia is still the same when it comes to caste system. There are lower and upper class, untouchability, the difference between man and woman, etc.

The caste system is the biggest problem in the growth of any country or region, there have been numerous methods used to eradicate it but the results have not been as expected. What is that we are missing right from the beginning? We have failed to understand the ***"One Soul One God" concept.***

How to understand that and how to make people believe in it is a big question. But we have a solution hidden in our scriptures and holy books but we don't want to implement. From Bhagwat Gita to Quran to Bible to Shri Guru Granth Saheb Ji all say only one thing, there is one God who created the whole of this universe and all humans are souls.

We need to look at each other as souls and not as human bodies, we need to understand who we are and why we are. Today people believe in materialistic things instead of spiritual. To revamp this mindset we need to follow the age-old technique that is Meditation and yoga.

We need to convince people to Meditate and do yoga because when you meditate you become one with yourself. There is a simple concept in meditation, ***"This whole universe is from you and you are from this whole universe"***. That's the point to understand and it's not that difficult with continuous practice of meditation. Government of India is working towards making yoga global and trying to bring more and more people to do yoga.

But only this much won't be enough, we need to reach to every individual and convince them for Meditation, that's the only way to do it. We can open meditation centers in every area same as mohalla clinics in Delhi, where people can easily walk in and meditate in the presence of guide or mentor. There are a lot of people who would be ready to volunteer for it. We can also arrange open public programs for it. Like in my city every Sunday, there is an event organized by Local Municipal body called Matargashti where people have fun, play games, do different activities and meditate. This helps in bringing people closer to each other and remove their differences.

In a diversified country like India, there is only one way for people to come together, through these public events where we can push people for Meditation. We have seen people going around in for the same, which is wonderful. "*Well begin is half done*" so Meditate, meditate and meditate that's the key to being one with yourself and this universe and it is through only by this way that people will realize that there is only one caste that is humanism.

"One Soul One God" is not just a concept but a reality which everyone needs to understand.

-Mandeep Singh Chawla

Honor killing

India being a secular country, is tolerant in many social evils. One such evil that is plunging our society for two centuries is caste. This evil practice has destroyed our society like a plague. To uphold the caste pride, Honor killing is implemented in our society for a long time. Even though it is considered illegal by our constitution, it is widely practiced even today.

Honor killing is an action done by the parents whose daughter or son indulge in Inter-caste love marriage. This barbaric act has drank the blood of innocent young people all India for a long time. This should be immediately taken into account on emergency bases and should be eradicated from our civilized society. This evil act is not brought in front of the Law often. This criminal offenders escape from this evil act in the name of caste or Religion. They are treated like heroes in their community and often portrayed as Semi - God, who is upholding their caste value. This type of glorifying an individual leads to communal fight among the people. Government should come forward to eradicate this inhuman act by implementing strict laws. Educated youths of our country should step forward to erase this maniac by dropping their surname and encourage inter-Caste marriage. Educational institutions must educate the future citizens about a

Tamil saying, **"One race, One God"** (ஒன்றே குலம் , ஒருவனே தெவன்) theory, which stress that we all belong to one race i.e., Human Race, we are ruled by one God and there should be no difference among us. Life is a precious gift from nature and no one has the right to take it away giving out any reasons for it. Life is full of learning curves and people should learn from their mistakes and Honor killing is not a solution for the mistake done by the young couples. They can be educated on the need to be self disciplined and taking responsibility to lead the way for the future Generations. An educated society will always have a diplomatic way for solving a problem and all the children of our country should be educated on caste system and the steps needed to eradicate it as soon as possible. The evil branches of the caste system are spreading in our society lately like a wildfire. Honor killing is one such evil daughter of caste system that is making a bigger threat to our country's sovereignty. It should be put to rest as soon as possible. Let us take a pledge that we all will come together to throw away this Practice from our society and make our future Generations a happy family.

-Bala Sundaram . P

Indian Caste System

The building of the Caste system in India is thousands of years old which is definitely the biggest obstacle in the path of progressing India, but nothing is impossible in this high tech era.

We are all different seeds in this world, being processed to be bloomed into a complete flower and lately exit from the earth after showering the beauty of our scent, but at last, we all are seeds only. I believe that there are only three crucial beings superior to us, our parents, our gurus, and the all-mighty god. If there are only these three considered as the premium ones then why not we all remain at the basic level and try to co-operate with each other?

No, but this is not the case in India, there is one more seed sowed by us thousands of years before with its roots spread in the whole country. The problem of untouchability, inter-caste marriage, distinction into Scheduled caste, Scheduled tribes, etc. are the major roots. What can we do to remove these roots? The golden dirt of the caste system rubbed on themselves by every individual should be brushed off.

Starting from the youngest member of the family who is the future of our country, they should remain free of this golden dust. Every human has its own right to live their life according to their will and we have no right to intervene in their business. Our family members are our priority but let us not forget the role of humanity. This wild disease of the caste system can be eradicated if we all take the vaccination of love to spread the light of joy and happiness. Let us help the government to implement whatever good they want to by cooperating with them and behaving like mature citizens. We all should understand one thing that this caste thing is man-made and not composed by the god. Believe in yourself and god by which you can conquer the universe.

Those innocents who die because of this wild disease are the victims but their place in the dwelling of God will be the eternal heaven and their assassins will pay for their sins in the same birth. Choose your place - *heaven or hell ?*

Let us imagine a better India and implement our imagination to make our country a better place to live in with everyone deserving a smiling face.

-Shivani khemani

Equal rights to all Caste

From a long time humans have divided the world into caste, Humans follow different caste and they fight for the same with many other human sayings he is the best, doing this way The world will really change? We must say no! Once you give equal respect and equal rights to all caste then the world will change. Equal rights should be given to each human living in this world, one person doesn't make the nation, all are family in this world.

We also know that there are many different places where different religion persons offer prayer to god. Some worship Jesus, Allah, and many different gods. Humanity has divided into various caste where different peoples are killed on the name of it, some plays politics in the name of caste so that they can rule the nation.

Do you think we are the ones due to which caste has made in this world?

Yes, we humans for our greed we do such things so we can be top in this world, just for some money we murder some person, for money we file a false complaint and many such things are happening due to us. If we go like this way there will be a time where every house will be divided into the caste saying high-level caste get more respect then lower caste.

Due to us government provide cheap rate things to lower caste but we still take their chance and put our selves into lower caste and get jobs and many other things. Due to no equality in caste, the person who deserves the job doesn't get the job, the person who deserves all things, he/she wants doesn't get that thanks to us. The one person who has good money Their kids still study at a very cheap rate, the one who does a lot of hard work still don't get what he wants and does suicide all these occur due to us.

Also, our media does the same thing if a low caste person is harassed they show telecast for a number of time while for others they don't care. Are we humans that question always stuck in one's mind when they do a lot of hard work and don't get what they want. We will face many problems giving every person equal rights giving what they deserve then what they want in the name of caste. We can stop all this if we want, just get up from the dream and giving the right person what they deserve. Stop politics in the name of caste we are tired of it we want the world to be one family not to be different children's of one parent who just want money, property, and rights and can do whatever to get it. If we want everyone has equal right to stop judging people on the basis of caste. If we can we could change the world and make a family where everyone is given equal opportunity what they want.

-Mohan sharma

Caste doesn't Unite Us, It just separates us

Hold on to people, problems don't see caste and barge in. When in need, even a small leaf can be helpful which can save a life. Basically, caste is just another tag to differentiate between people. Having knowledge doesn't mean you know everything, but being in a particular caste, means you get everything for either free or half-price than others.

Caste has its place even in the educational system of our country. The fees paid by general category is more and paid by others is exactly half or one fourth. The fees which they cannot pay is collected from us as if we belong to the Rich families of the history. Why is it so no one has understood till date.

When everyone has the right to education, why the fees paid by different categories should vary?

The caste system has to be eradicated totally.

It can be eradicated by:

1. Setting the same fee payment structure.

2. Educating everyone about how the caste differentiation creates barricades in the society outside.

3. Throwing light on what destruction the caste system does to the mentality of people.

4. The eradication of caste system, teaches students how to treat everyone equally in the world outside.

5. Setting the same cut off percentages in educational institutions.

6. Treating them equal without giving them any special allowances.

7. Accepting them the way they are.

8. For the students to learn, first the teacher's should be made aware of the unity which castes seem to break.

9. Hiring the talented teachers/lecturers/staff members in the educational institutions.

10. Giving salary/allowances etc. based on the designation, hard work, talents, etc. and not based on caste.

Once the caste system is eradicated, everyone will be treated as one, equally. We should learn that Caste basically just splits us into parts which isn't good for the society. we will be happier without castes and barriers of caste. Caste doesn't unite us, it just splits us instead which is why we fall apart very easily.

-Deeksha R. Adiga

India being a vast country has a long history of Eradication of Caste system. From prehistory, many people played an important role in the eradication of caste. In ancient India, many of them like Gautama Buddha, Mahaveer contributed. In the modern period, Eminent personalities like Jyotiba Phule, Dr. B.R. Ambedkar and many others did much for the nation to be discrimination-free.

Jyotiba Phule stated that the origin of the caste system lies in racial conflict.

Dr. B.R. Ambedkar, our constitution maker, deeply thought about the change to be made in society.

His main concept was on – **ANNIHILATE CASTE**. He started with awarding the society about the principles of religion. He stated a complete change in the fundamental notions of life. He thought of conversion of religion means new life.

The most important measure to be taken to eradicate caste system from society is educating the society about the Ethics and a deep study has to be taken on **ARTICLE-15** which states prohibition on discrimination of caste, race, religion, sex or place of birth. Lack of education makes people more superstitious and mythical which is now a day leading us to a drawback.

Political Background

No one ignores SC/ ST and backward castes, including those from among Muslims, as they have almost 70% share of the electorate. Till the time, we have the right to vote, no one can get a side to this pannel. The root of this is "*one person one vote*" in our parliamentary democracy. This was the biggest equalizer that Baba saheb Ambedkar gifted our nation. Reservation for the Dalits was introduced to ensure there was no injustice done to them and to bring them to mainstream and uphold the legacy.

Many government policies have been implemented as the cast hierarchy differed from one religion to another. Specially *NGO's* have a great role in the eradication of the caste system. They should try to stop the violence against the Dalits. They can conduct seminars, workshops or street plays to enhance more equality towards the casteism.

Media Impact

More books and articles should be written against discrimination and to ensure that the caste system is slowly annihilated, as these mass media have a huge cultural impact on society and its development.

There should be no use of the word CASTE because the word itself states inequality and disharmony. So, this can affect more to the new generation as they do not differentiate and are open-minded. More encouragement should be given to Inter-caste marriages. Not only the couple but the family should also unite and enlighten more onto the fact. This will grow more impact and different caste should be able to understand each other.

Casteism can be removed if the new outlook in mind of people can be developed.

-Rubal Choudhary

To Eradicate All, Create One

India is a land of diversity, where people belonging to several religions and castes, speaking different languages live together. But instead of promoting unity in diversity (as it is preached to be), the country has led itself to be divided by them. Riots, honor killing, bomb blasts, and several massacres are born from such divisions that seem to rule the country. There might be several ways to battle this rotten disease of the caste system that has been infecting the land for a long time. But the first and foremost step will be to unite all those who are against it into one single band, so that they can fight together against the malice practice and establish the true meaning of "Unity in Diversity".

Thus, the main aim is to create one singular group of such people who are against the caste system. Let's call the group **Naste**, as in No Caste equals **Naste**. Anybody, who believes in equality, can be a member of the group, no matter which caste or religion they belong to. No separate rules will pertain to the members of the Naste, they can continue with whatever belief they are born with or can even choose a new one if they want. But each member will have to promise one thing that they will never judge another person based on their caste or religion. Theist, Atheist, Hindu, Muslim, Christian, Brahmin, Scheduled Caste, etc. all are welcomed in Naste so long as they don't try to impose their beliefs upon another.

Although the members will be allowed to preach about Naste to aware people of its existence, they can't force someone to be a member of it. Even if they want, they can't—for there won't be any system of formal baptism to convert a person into being a Naste follower. It's only the inner belief of equality that will make one join the venture.

The creation of Brahmo Samaj back in the nineteen century failed to spread its effectiveness because it had its own sets of tight rules and regulations that didn't allow any flexibility. Of course, it liberated the people of the shackles of the plagued system that prevailed then but was unsuccessful in attracting more people towards the movement because many were not ready to abandon the set of beliefs they were born with and accept the ones that Brahmo Samaj offered. Thus, even though Brahmo Samaj was created on a logical base, it failed to appeal to the mass: for when it comes to beliefs, people tend to consider through their heart and not the brain.

Naste will, however, negate this aspect of the Brahmo Samaj. It will not set any restrictions on the followers, except for the promise of looking at each other equally. When people will have nothing to lose, but only the promise of gaining equality despite their caste or religious beliefs, they would surely join the venture to eradicate the caste system and contribute towards creating a better India.

-Sanchari Das

Eradicate casteism : A Big threat

Casteism is discrimination on grounds of case. In ancient times, caste was divided on the basis of occupation, the principle of birth but then came the self-proclaimed god-men who misinterpreted Vedas and unpunished. They preached one cannot change their occupation and created hierarchy based on occupation (toady known as caste) eliminating casteism is not easy as it's 2000 years old tradition but we can mitigate debilitating effects on our society, the people of low Caste are treated as polluted caste or outcaste redistribution of land: almost 70% of SC/ST have less than 2.5 acres of landholding compared to 28.9% of general. Also, previous land distribution program largely failed.

Section 123A of representation act clear mention that use of caste, religion, and language to appeal voters is electoral offense, here I would like to mention the role of OBC politics in 2014 the departure of BJP from erstwhile Hindutva to OBC politics depicts the cauterization of politics and politicization of caste. Everybody is aware of such politics prevalent in India. Caste equation is used to win the election for instance in UP, SP calculates the number of.

The use of word DALIT in itself derogatory when Ram Nath Kovind becomes president, social media depicted him as first DALIT President. So social media should use such words cautiously. Vinay Kodare has given a good example regarding blunder made by social media Irony is DALIT word which was once used to call the lower section had become their identity.All say is stop judging people on their appearance, name, caste, color, sex, education. Be the change if you want to see changes in the world. Stop hating people. Be the human, not a racism.

Merely reading answers won't eliminate casteism. Let's pledge for new India being floated by honorable PM.

-Siddharth Sharma

The Temple of Caste

India a country of vivid culture, different traditions, religion, beliefs and people from different caste, well out of all this difference, the caste is the only word which triggers everyone's mind whenever they read it. Caste system in India is more complex than what it actually looks like or it was made. This system of caste which is prevailing in India from decades actually emerged in the Vedic period. When this caste system was created for the betterment of the society but then this system changed into a set of code of conduct for the society and people from the higher caste used this system as per their wants and just started the era of misleading and hazardous things on the lower caste people including violence in the latter part of it. This with time resulted in rigorous fights and caste wars which divided the society instead of uniting it. In this article, I would be talking about the issue of Temple entry restrictions on lower caste people specifically as this issue is very serious and all the other caste-related issues according to me is in a way related to this. So temple, as we all know, is a holy worship place for prayers which is done by Hindus and they come there to pray to god and wish for a better life and future, the importance of temple is written in many of the mythological books of Hindus and temples have been found as much as from Indus valley civilization and later eras too. Now the main issue what arises was lower caste people have not been allowed to go into the temple just because they belong to lower caste and higher caste people use to beat them and harass them if they try to do, the problem is so serious that lower caste peoples life is made as if they are in a war without guns and ammo and where they could not even speak. One of the most important reasons for these things to get worse at such a stage is lack of education for the lower caste people without education they don't know what are their rights and what they can actually do to come out of this vicious circle where their generations and generations are trapped into. People after facing such tremendous issues outside can not even enter temple and worship and pray to God which within itself is a grave thing.

This problem can be eradicated only with education also other problems which are related to the caste system in India could be solved with education as when people get educated they start thinking in a different way and this results in a change of behavior of them. If we look in the 19th century and back the lower caste people were less educated and the problems associated with them were very high and various types of harassment were done on them and many were killed, the number has drastically come down in 2019 and if we see the records lower caste people are getting educated more and so the main link in eradication of caste and the caste system itself is education. When all get educated people will transfer all the good things and all those mature thinking into the new youth which would result in slowly eradication of the negative thinking of the society against the lower caste and with time the concept of cast itself might end up leading to a better future for our next generation who would live in a caste free India.

-Ankur payar

Caste can be cruel

Coming to reality, we all know that we are divided on the basis of caste and religions, which has got highs and lows.

Though we all are human, God's children, but we are treated differently on the basis of our caste.
If you belong to a higher caste, you are treated with respect while if you belong to a lower caste, you are hardly respected. But then if you belong to a lower caste, you get more seats in the reservation system, and if you belong to higher caste you get fewer seats in the reservation system.
There is a lot of discrimination we have been facing due to caste. Everyone knows about the issue, but does anyone have any solution? Think about it.
When you fall in love with someone, you don't check whether he or she belongs to your caste, culture. You don't even check his/her financial status, as those things don't matter to you anymore. But it still does matter to our society, and for them, it matters a lot.

Even in 2019, people prohibit inter-caste marriages. However, it is gradually gaining acceptance due to education, but still, it's ratio is less than twenty-five-percent.

Let me give you an idea, as it is said, if you want to remove the problem, then cut it from the roots. So as we all know about the process called "adoption". Where parents or a capable individual can adopt a child. And for your information, the children to be adopted belongs to no caste and religion. Those children don't have any tag on them. They are just little children and while adopting, no one even cares what caste or religion the child is from. So when a child can be adopted without any discrimination and brought up with love and care, then why can't this be implied in other cases. Why can't our society allow an inter-caste marriage?

What I mean to say is that caste doesn't make any difference, it's the society who have made it, it only exists in our brain. Before expecting others to understand this, you should understand it first. Because if you will get it right, your society will start getting it as you are part of society.

We need to eradicate caste because it is only leading to discrimination, which further leads to fighting, and a country where people fight with each other over pity things, can never become a developed nation. We need to stand for each other, only then the individual growth is possible, which will help in educating the society and ending this social evil which has been eating our nation for centuries.

-Amrita singh

Laws: Use and Misuse

Post-independence India saw a lot of aggression and violence on caste-based communalism. Although we are well into the 21st century, this still seems prevalent. So the questions arise: What is the real problem? Why is caste still something we talk about? How are laws not made to improve the situation? If they are, then how aren't they implemented? Let's delve a little deeper.

Law, A highly broad term, so to say. The Constitution of India has various laws written under articles. To help with the disparity among the castes, and to uplift the situation of lower castes, there were many laws passed.

Article 14: Equality before law.

Article 17: Abolition of untouchability.

Article 15(5): Provision for Reservation of Backward, SC and ST classes in private educational institutions.

Prevention of Atrocities Act, 1989: An Act to prevent the commission of offences of atrocities against the members of the Scheduled Castes and the Scheduled Tribes, to provide for Special Courts for the trial of such offences and for the relief and rehabilitation of the victims of such offences and for matters connected therewith or incidental thereto. and many more such laws.

But what do we see in reality?

In rural areas, untouchability is still practiced, where at shops or eateries, people of upper castes refuse to use vessels used by people of lower castes. Even in public places like temples, lower caste people are not allowed to enter. Also, there are many cases mostly in villages, where the police guard the door to justice. They vehemently refuse to file FIRs for incidents such as harassment or rape of women of lower castes, caste-based labor wage malpractices under the PoA Act, 1989.

In urban areas, however, the scenario can be seen in reverse. For admissions in educational institutions, a lot of people of lower castes produce caste certificates based on fake income documents, and hence procure seats they don't deserve. Even in government jobs, people of lower castes easily get access to higher posts, compared to those of the upper castes. In cities, there have been incidents of false accusations under the PoA Act, 1989. In residential areas or commercial spaces, there have been cases of lower caste people misusing the Act, to take advantage of the situation they are in.

How can these problems be solved?

The absolute ideal way to solve the problem is for the government to dissolve the entire caste system altogether, and make it a criminal offense even to mention it. But that's easier said than done.

Laws should be made or amended focusing more on equality, rather than prejudice. Instead of accepting lower castes as backward and then taking action for their upliftment, the laws can be made by showing a void in the equality system, and that the lower castes should fill that void.

A task force can be set up working only under the jurisdiction of the Supreme Court, which will review the documents regarding admissions in institutions, and check for legitimacy. Similarly, task forces can be set up in rural areas, which will oversee the working of the police, and make sure they work in accordance with the law.

As commoners, people can spread awareness on how the caste system has become cancer for the country, and how we can take measures on uprooting it.

-Siddhesh Shimpukade

Eradication of Caste

Caste; community; unit; group; section and department is a result of clear discrimination.

They are made for making different groups lead in community. They are making different rules which are not really related and practical with the actual word.

In India there is some community which made for reserve some seats in India legislation such as OPEN; another backward caste: Scheduled tribes; Scheduled Caste which are differentiated for development of lower cast for getting jobs in government.

Actually, in the constitution this contract was allowed for only next 50 years but it's still going to upgrade in rules due to this most of lower cast are getting government jobs easily and taking benefits of all schemes. In another side, those who are in open and obc categories still have to do struggle for all this. After getting 80/150 there are not get the job and 55/150 are deserving of the job.

It is clear discrimination of caste discrimination of community. And It should be eradicated from society so everyone can get what they deserved.

-Vishal Bhatiya

Third Gender: The Outcaste of our Society

The Indian society is divided into various sects and classes this is because of the caste system which is prevalent in the country. And casteism in India is the most heated topic for debates. There are many sections of societies living in India according to this ancient arrangement, having their respective place in social system ranked according to their caste, but still there is one section of the society that is still looking for its place in our culture, they don't have any caste but still they are the outcaste of our society. They are the Third Gender most often called as **'kinner'** or **'Hizra'**.

Trans genders are often discarded by their own families and are rejected from the societies as well. Lack of access to education and non-availability of jobs forces them to beg. Dressed in glittering sarees, their faces heavily coated in cheap makeup, they sashay through crowded intersections knocking on car windows with the edge of a coin and offering blessings. They dance at temples. They crash fancy weddings and birth ceremonies, singing bawdy songs and leaving with fistfuls of rupees. Behind the theatrics are often sad stories — of the sex trade and exploitation, cruel and dangerous castrations, being cast out and constantly humiliated.

One of the most common prejudices present in society is ***"Being The Parent Of A Transgender Child Is Shameful"***, because of which people disown their own children to suffer alone in this world – it's heartbreaking!.

The transgender community is one of the most marginalized communities in the country because they do not fit into the general categories of the gender of 'male' or 'female'. Consequently, they face problems ranging from social exclusion to discrimination, lack of education facilities, unemployment, lack of medical facilities and so on.

According to the study by the National Human Rights Commission, the total population of trans genders according to the 2011 Census is 4.8 lakh; only 30,000 are registered with the Election Commission. However, estimates suggest there are 50 to 60 lakh trans genders in India but most keep it a secret to avoid discrimination. Around 99 percent have suffered social rejection on more than one occasion, including from their family while 96 percent of trans genders are denied jobs and are forced to take low paying works. 50 to 60 percent of trans genders have never attended schools and faced discrimination. Around 57 percent are keen on getting sex-alignment surgery but don't have money for it. 18 percent of them are physically abused, 62 percent are verbally abused in school. 15 percent are harassed by students as well as teachers.

Meanwhile, violence against women in India has gained national attention – millions protested against sexual assault after a student was gang-raped in Delhi in 2012 – But country's transgender community says they still feel that crimes against them stay largely hidden in the shadows.

India sees a furor every time there's a rape case, but not for the trans genders. When a transgender woman gets raped, even the cops first mock her, saying she doesn't have the organs to be sexually assaulted, and what follows is a barrage of injustices.

While Prostitution "is a given" for hijras. Hijra sex workers sell themselves for 30 to 50 rupees. They don't have any other option except begging but still, they lack in earning to sustain their life.

They are also humans, part of our democracy, citizens of the nation but it took 67 long years by our constitution to give them legal status. In a landmark judgment in 2014, the Supreme Court observed that "The transgender community, generally known as "Hijras" in this country, are a section of Indian citizens who are treated by the society as *"unnatural and generally as objects of ridicule and even fear on account of superstition"*. In its judgment, the Supreme Court passed the ruling that *"In view of the constitutional guarantee, the transgender community is entitled to basic rights i.e. Right to Personal Liberty, dignity, Freedom of expression, Right to Education and Empowerment, Right against violence, discrimination and exploitation, and Right to work. Moreover, every person must have the right to decide his/her gender expression and identity, including transsexuals, trans genders, hijras and should have right to freely express their gender identity and be considered as a third sex."*

But still, there are so many hurdles in the path of getting equal rights for this community. The reality is that the Transgender Rights Bill 2014, which was passed in Rajya Sabha, but was later deformed and later introduced in Lok Sabha in 2016 by present BJP government has not been passed yet. The attitude of politicians towards trans has been that of hypocrisy. Politicians who use Indian citizens as vote banks feel uneasy to bring any positive change in society due to the fear of losing votes. Thus even when India is a democratic and so-called inclusive country, the fate of the minorities is left in the hands of the majority, which often creates more hurdles.

This is the harsh reality for almost every trans people in India. But the fact we often ignore or don't even realize is that directly or indirectly, we, as a society, are responsible for their condition. Many hijras feel a sense of alienation, of being looked at as freaks. And this will continues until or unless the government as well as the society brings new laws to protect the laws of the trans genders and opens its hands to accept them as a part of society and culture.

Economy vs caste

Definition of caste and economy doesn't have any similarity but like every single leaf of a tree branch is important for a tree, just like that economy is leafless without the eradication of caste. Yes, *Casteism can be seen in every hierarchical aspect of the economy* because people's mindsets are set as per they are taught by there elders, but in reality nor economy nor even caste is separating our society.

Those myths of Casteism aren't myths anymore, we can feel, and observe it in our daily life, in school, in office, on streets, in short at every place. Schools are made for education, skill development, and building confidence, it doesn't matter school is government or private but these all are just sayings, high standard schools to low standard villages, nor city nor villages but the whole economy is discriminated, we all are trying to pull each other back and climb the heights of success alone.

Casteism should be depleted to develop an individual, his esteem and his dreams, there shouldn't be any boundaries for an individual, everyone should be given proper and equal rights to fly in the sky, to smile but not deny, to make a mark on peek, do not fall like an unwinged butterfly.

The economy includes everything within itself from individual to whole country's growth and development and that growth and development can only be achieved if proper education, opportunities, and facilities are provided but is this really possible with the existence of such hate in people due to Casteism, untouchability, backward class and so on.

When a child starts growing from his early childhood stage, he becomes a very important part of our economy, our society but what we taught him, don't talk to that black child in the park, or that poor child of a neighbor, is that right? Will he be able to evaluate what is all this going on? No, not at all but just like a puppet he too will start copying what he is been taught.

I think some people are hiding from there own reality, they are not able to accept where they belong to and they don't even have guts to say that loudly or take a stand because they are not given many teachings, they are bought up like this, they are not taught such values related to there caste, is that hurting you? But the truth is bitter right? In life everything, every single thing is so beautiful then why don't we think caste as a beautiful thing like God has given us different look, color, weight and height, then why don't caste? Why can't we look caste as just like different shades of red, different color of eyes of two different people?

There are many things which are unacceptable but with time they settle in our lives like they were never separate.

The economy is from people and people are from the economy, God has gifted us a structure which is primary and that structure is divided into different body parts, different bones. Just like that our economy is a gift by society and in which people are merged into small groups which they named community but further those communities are divided into different castes and negativity immersed in it. Some rules and regulations were made by the government to give a helping to those who are needy, as they give 10% reservation to lower backward caste, but was that decision right? Poor can be in every caste People aren't backward by there caste but are by the economy.

People aren't backward by there community but are by locality. People aren't backward by thoughts but are by what they are taught. But no one took real steps for eradication of caste, because people(you, yes you) are still discussing on such topic but are ignoring it in reality, we all are dividing our country into partitions and making our economy weak by ourselves, with lack of awareness. *Eradicate caste built a better economy, a better society and a better place to live.*

-Risha Jagga

Casteism: In the view of the 21st century

Caste is India's badge. Nowadays when I think about a superior society my mind scramble and let me remind that evilness spreads for the cast system in our motherland. In our past, the great leaders of independent India have paid tribute to this system. Yet, India's caste-based society preserves and values social diversity. As our history tell us 'Caste is not the basic expression of the Indian tradition. In modern India, the term caste is used for "jaat" and also for large and that is used by the British who ruled our mother Nation until 1947. The British who wanted to rule India efficiency made lists of Indian communities. They used two terms to describe Indian communities castes and trades.

The main problem is in the rural areas the people of cities and the well-developed town has started to become flexible in their caste system custom. In general, the urban people in India are less strict about this system then the rural. It is the story of my childhood when the surrounding made me realize about that thing that I never came across. So here the story begins when I was in 4th standard I used to visit my grandparent's native place that was not so well developed at that time and that place made me aware about the discrimination based on caste and sometimes also untouchability. My grandmother, she always told me in clear words and always reminded me not to touch any of lower caste or if I touched, she used to force me to take a bath in that days of winter's evening but this is undone. Our society must stand with us to put such things a full stop.

As a responsible citizen of our modern society, it is our responsibility to stop this type of awareness among the people of our country and let them realize about the power of unity and brotherhood starting up with small things can help us achieve the goal of Unity. To make our country our mother Nation a better place for our future generation, we should educate the upcoming generation to pull up by the roots to up of this system. As the sun spreads light the beautiful of brightness among the whole world without asking our caste, Creed, color, religion then who am I to do such things If this kind of thinking takes place in the hearts of each an every Indian then only our next generation can live a respectful life in pride.

-Vaishno singh

ABOUT SPREAD SMILE

Spread Smile is a platform founded by Shruti Tayal. It deals with anthologies, providing a platform to all the budding writers across the globe for getting published. It helps them to showcase their talents to get recognized in the society.

Our main objective is to spread smile among everyone. In the race of spreading smile, we have published our first anthology "Petals of Life" in which 60+ writers have been published successfully.

If you have sparks and want to get published in anthologies like "Eradication of Caste" then contact us via-

Email: spreadsmile28@gmail.com

Instagram: @__spread.smile__

Spread Smile

You can contact the Publisher at:

www.fanatixx.in